Water Everywhere!

Written by Christine Taylor-Butler   Illustrated by Maurie J. Manning

Children's Press®
A Division of Scholastic Inc.
New York • Toronto • London • Auckland • Sydney
Mexico City • New Delhi • Hong Kong
Danbury, Connecticut

Dear Parents/Educators,

Welcome to Rookie Ready to Learn. Each Rookie Reader in this series includes additional age-appropriate Let's Learn Together activity pages that help your young child to be better prepared when starting school. *Water Everywhere!* offers opportunities for you and your child to talk about the important social/emotional skill of **development of self: natural curiosity**.

Here are early-learning skills you and your child will encounter in the *Water Everywhere!* Let's Learn Together pages:

- Rhyming
- Vocabulary
- Science: sink or float?

We hope you enjoy sharing this delightful, enhanced reading experience with your early learner.

Library of Congress Cataloging-in-Publication Data

Taylor-Butler, Christine.
  Water everywhere! / written by Christine Taylor-Butler ; illustrated by Maurie J. Manning.
    p. cm. -- (Rookie ready to learn)
  ISBN 978-0-531-26504-8 – ISBN 978-0-531-26736-3 (pbk.)
  1. Water--Juvenile literature. I. Manning, Maurie, ill. II. Title. III. Series.
  GB662.3.T43 2011
  553.7--dc22
                        2010050003

It's morning!
Time to start my day.

I wash my face before I play.

I brush my teeth in the sink.

I give my lizard fresh water to drink.

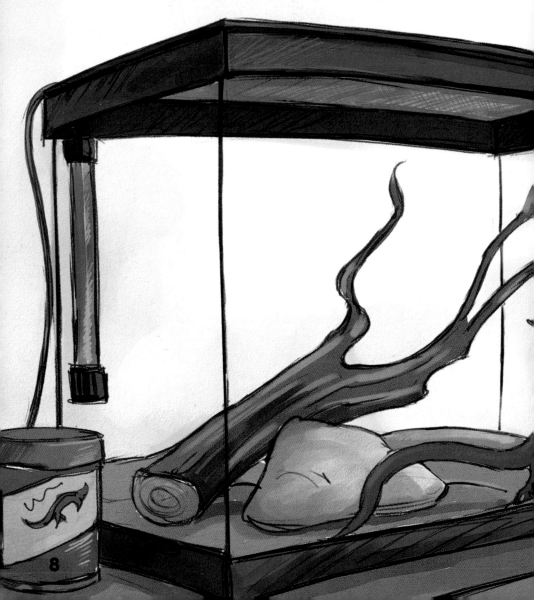

I make a batch of lemonade.

I put flowers in the vase I made.

13

I make rainbows with
the garden hose.

I watch the clouds.
What shapes are those?

Uh oh! I feel raindrops.

I splash in every puddle around.

I see my reflection on the ground.

I come inside and fill the tub.

I make lots of bubbles.
Time to scrub.

I'd still be out if not for the rain.

Tomorrow I will start again.

Congratulations!

You just finished reading *Water Everywhere!* and saw all the ways in which you need water.

About the Author

Christine Taylor-Butler is an explorer at heart and loves playing in the water.

About the Illustrator

Maurie J. Manning is the author and illustrator of a 2004 International Reading Association's Notable Book, and has illustrated many other books.

We Need the Rain

(Sing this song to the tune of "It's Raining, It's Pouring.")

It's raining, it's pouring.
The people are snoring.
The rain goes in the ground
and the flowers say "thanks."
So we play in the rain all
morning.

It's dripping, it's dropping.
We keep on hopping.
The rain pitters and patters
while birds take their baths.
And in puddles we'll jump —
We're not stopping!

PARENT TIP: Discussing *Water Everywhere!* is a wonderful way to explore the importance of water. Explain that all living things need water. Plants need it to grow and stay healthy, and so do we! Talk with your child about how your family uses water and the ways in which you work to save, or conserve, water — such as turning off the faucet when you brush your teeth.

Lemonade Fun

The little girl in the story used water to make lemonade for her teddy bear. Her teddy bear is thirsty! Follow the path of things she used to make the lemonade.

Cloud Gazing

The girl liked to watch clouds and find different shapes. Look at the clouds and then look at each picture. Point to each cloud and picture that look alike. Can you also find the cloud that is shaped like a heart ♥ ?

dinosaur   chick

star

PARENT TIP: Watching clouds is a relaxing and creative way to spend time on a nice day outdoors! Go outside with your child and look at the clouds. What do you both see? To prompt discussion, you can say, "I see a cloud that looks like a circle," or ask, "Can you find the littlest cloud?"

37

Water Everywhere

The little girl discovered a lot of amazing things about water. When she drank water, it was a liquid. When she put ice into the glass, water was a solid. When she looked at the clouds, she was looking at water as vapor, or gas. Water comes in three forms: liquid, solid, and vapor.

Look at the pictures below. Point to water in its solid form. Point to water in its vapor form. Point to water in its liquid form.

liquid

solid

vapor

Sink or Float?

The little girl likes her rubber duckie because it can float. In water, things can either sink or float. How do you know which things will sink and which will float? Try this experiment.

YOU WILL NEED: **Large, clear plastic container filled with water** **Objects such as soap** **, rock, sponge, leaf, penny, crayon, plastic straw**

1 **Pick up an object. Do you think it will sink or float?**

2 **Put it in water. What happens?**

3 **Repeat with each object.**

PARENT TIP: Learning new science concepts promotes a strong curiosity. Encourage your child's natural curiosity and early scientific understanding by giving her opportunities such as this activity to experiment and have fun making predictions.

Water Everywhere! Word List (72 Words)

a	for	not	teeth
again	fresh	of	the
and	garden	oh	those
are	give	on	time
around	ground	out	to
batch	hose	play	tomorrow
be	I	puddle	tub
before	I'd	put	uh
brush	if	rain	vase
bubbles	in	rainbows	wash
clouds	inside	raindrops	watch
come	it's	reflection	water
day	lemonade	scrub	what
drink	lizard	see	will
every	lots	shapes	with
face	made	sink	
feel	make	splash	
fill	morning	start	
flowers	my	still	

PARENT TIP: Take this opportunity to point out to your child that the author of *Water Everywhere!* wrote the story with words that rhyme, or have the same ending sound, such as *drink* and *sink*. Find the other words in the word list that rhyme and say them out loud with your child. Your child might enjoy going back through the book with you to find the words that rhyme.